蔡榮勇 著
Poems by Tsai Jung-Yung

陳郁青 英譯
Translated by Jean Chen

保坂登志子 日譯
Translated by Hosaka Tosiko

日記，謝謝你

Thank You Diary
日記よ、ありがとう

蔡榮勇漢英日三語詩集
Mandarin-English- Japanese

台灣詩叢 • Taiwan Poetry Series 17

保坂登志子來台旅遊照

日記，謝謝你

Thank you Diary・日記よ、ありがとう

【總序】詩推台灣意象

叢書策畫／李魁賢

　　進入21世紀，台灣詩人更積極走向國際，個人竭盡所能，在詩人朋友熱烈參與支持下，策畫出席過印度、蒙古、古巴、智利、緬甸、孟加拉、尼加拉瓜、馬其頓、秘魯、突尼西亞、越南、希臘、羅馬尼亞、墨西哥等國舉辦的國際詩歌節，並編輯《台灣心聲》等多種詩選在各國發行，使台灣詩人心聲透過作品傳佈國際間。

　　多年來進行國際詩交流活動最困擾的問題，莫如臨時編輯帶往國外交流的選集，大都應急處理，不但時間緊迫，且選用作品難免會有不週。因此，興起策畫【台灣詩叢】雙語詩系的念頭。若台灣詩人平常就有雙語詩集出版，隨時可以應用，詩作交流與詩人交誼雙管齊下，更具實際成效，對台灣詩的國際交流活動，當更加順利。

　　以【台灣】為名，著眼點當然有鑑於台灣文學在國際間名目不彰，台灣詩人能夠有機會在國際努力開拓空間，非為個人建立知名度，而是為推展台灣意象的整體事功，期待開創台灣文學的長久景象，才能奠定寶貴的歷史意義，台灣文學終必在世界文壇上佔有地位。

　　實際經驗也明顯印證，台灣詩人參與國際詩交流活動，很受

重視，帶出去的詩選集也深受歡迎，從近年外國詩人和出版社與本人合作編譯台灣詩選，甚至主動翻譯本人詩集在各國文學雜誌或詩刊發表，進而出版外譯詩集的情況，大為增多，即可充分證明。

　　承蒙秀威資訊科技公司一本支援詩集出版初衷，慨然接受【台灣詩叢】列入編輯計畫，對台灣詩的國際交流，提供推進力量，希望能有更多各種不同外語的雙語詩集出版，形成進軍國際的集結基地。

真味——序蔡榮勇《日記，謝謝你》

名評論家／林鷺

　　詩貴在詩人擁有一顆純淨的心，這也是詩人有時被人推崇是一種最接近神性的人。然而，我卻記得某位才氣橫溢的詩人卻曾感嘆過：「詩人其實一點也不單純。」因此，如果我們用純淨的詩心，來檢視詩存在的價值，我便會毫無疑慮的為詩人蔡榮勇這本寫作時間超過30年，由日本女詩人保坂登志子陸續翻譯的兒童詩集，感到無比的可貴與珍惜！

　　蔡榮勇長期經營兒童詩的園地，作品不在少數，保坂登志子則是一位熱心譯介台灣兒童詩的詩人，因此《日記，謝謝你》裡的這五十首，先後發表在日本《回聲》和《青色的地球》詩刊的詩作，我猜想以登志子對兒童詩豐富的經驗，應該是經由她篩選以後，才進行翻譯的作品，所以篇篇讀來都是上乘之作。

　　這本詩集的集結，作者並沒有就內容刻意加以分類，我大致可從以下幾個面向去賞閱這本詩集。

一、從日常生活引導兒童的觀察力

　　例如〈一粒白米飯〉內容就隱藏思慮珍惜米飯得來不易的內涵，但是表現的手法並無一絲說教的意味，只是單純引導兒童

思考，即使只是微小的一粒米飯，都具有可以飽足微小動物的價值，間接引導兒童產生珍惜物資得來不易的聯想；又如〈加法與減法〉一詩，也是以小朋友可以接受的親切語言，來引導善自珍惜時間做有用事情的重要；對於已經面臨成熟的孩童，則以下面這首：

〈轉大人〉
爬山的
爬
嬰兒學走路的
爬
爬山的心情
嬰兒學爬的心情

嬰兒爬久了
站起來
就會走路了
爬山，一步一步的
爬
爬上山頂

來激勵小朋友們「凡事只要按部就班，就能自然而然獲取最後成功」的詩作，都具有積極的啟發性意涵。

二、觸發兒童的同理心

　　「躺在床上／就會想到樹／／樹站了一天／腳會不會痠」
——〈床〉和「我會想／爺爺會不會寂寞／「奶奶會從天國回來
／陪他說話嗎？」——〈爺爺會不會寂寞〉，以及以下這首：

　　〈鞋子〉
　　他，歡樂
　　留下的汗珠
　　他，悲傷
　　留下的淚珠
　　他，緊張
　　留下的汗珠
　　他，運動
　　留下的汗珠

　　鞋子
　　一滴滴的收藏著
　　為了給她讀
　　讀出歲月的滋味

　　都是出自一種同理心的發想，也符合兒童生活現實的體驗。

三、激發愛與感恩的心

　　愛與感恩是人性一體兩面的可貴情懷。我們從「燭光　聆聽／夜黑黑的心聲／／燭光　打開夜黑黑的心靈」──〈燭〉裡的燭光愛心，和〈我是一粒籃球〉中「我是一粒籃球／看到小朋友／玩得開心／彈跳得　更開心」的樂於服務的籃球自述，以及「天地之間不會相撞／一定有一條線撐著」、「父母愛子女的心／一定有一條線撐著」──〈線〉中提醒子女對於父母的辛苦付出，理應心懷感恩，還有針對西元2011年日本東北大地震，引發強烈海嘯，導致福島核電廠核能外洩的災害所寫的詩作，都讓人看到一種溫暖如煦的愛與感同身受的同情心。

四、平常心與愛國心的啟示

　　如何面對人生起起伏伏的輸贏，自然是兒童教育很重要的一門功課，因此蔡榮勇以下這首：

　　〈乒乓球〉
　　一張桌子
　　一張網子
　　一雙拍子
　　一粒白球

雙方殺得眼花撩亂
汗流浹背

不管誰贏

一張桌子仍然一張桌子
一張網子仍然一張網子
一隻拍子仍然一隻拍子
一粒白球仍然一粒白球

　　讀起來好像很消極，實則是在對於人生無可避免，必然得面對各種輸贏的局面，所給予孩子們豁達的智慧性啟發。詩人最後透過一首以愛彩繪的〈Formosa〉，表達對於自己所生長的台灣、將伴隨一生的土地，其不渝的愛來做為詩集結束的詩章，是非常具有意義的感性表達，相信對於小朋友也必然會產生自由揮灑豐富色彩的感染力。

　　除此之外，詩人蔡榮勇當然也沒有忽略詩發揮在物象轉換的想像意趣，這在小朋友純真的世界裡，是上帝恩賜給生命最美的禮物。很多成年人寫詩給兒童，就是因為內在老早遺失了生命初始的純淨，所以經常呈現不忍卒讀的語境而不自知，實在非常可惜！然而，我們從〈笛子〉、〈西瓜〉、〈皺紋〉和〈大樹〉等詩作，都讀到了一種和兒童十分貼近的心境，這些詩姑且留待讀者慢慢去品味。

　　蔡榮勇與我同年，我們相互之間有多年詩友的交情，因之讓我有足夠的時間，從內心感受他與人相處的熱善，讚嘆他始終如常的至性純良。最特別的是，他不得失於名利爭逐的個性，坦白說，的確是世間少見！一個看似平凡應對人世，以致容易被人淡淡忽視的詩人身影，正好可以藉由這本來自時間累積而成的詩人形象，所描繪出最凸顯真味的詩，來做為詩人最接近神性品質的見證。

2021/1/18

感謝的話

　　台日交流，女詩人保坂登志子（1937-）為台灣兒童詩翻譯，在《回聲》和《青色的地球》發表，包括大人和兒童（為兒童和大人寫給兒童的詩）。

　　大約從1990年到2019年陸陸續續翻譯拙詩，統計結果一共有50首，其它有沒有遺漏不知道。

　　不懂日語的我，非常慚愧，她總是寫著一手端正秀麗的中文信給我。她來台灣拜訪大約四次之多，每次見面互相用手寫中文溝通。每次下定決心學日文，往往半途而廢。

　　為了感謝她的厚愛，結集出版表達微薄的感謝之意。

感謝的人

感謝詩人　保坂登志子

感謝詩人　李魁賢

感謝詩人　林鷺

感謝英譯者　陳郁青

感謝日譯者　李欣怡（序、中英簡介）

感謝編輯　陳彥儒

感謝內人　賴秀菊的支持

感謝附小校長　張友森的支持與鼓勵

感謝　田尾、實小國小學生的啟發

感謝　秀威出版社

目次

16

日記，謝謝你

Thank you Diary・日記よ、ありがとう

日記，謝謝你

日記，謝謝你！
你容忍，自私的我
你安慰，悲傷的我
你包容，生氣的我
你讚美，快樂的我
⋯⋯
日記，謝謝你！
收藏了
真實的我

一粒白米飯

一粒白米飯
幾十隻螞蟻才抬得動
我一餐
要吃好幾千粒的
白米飯
幾十隻螞蟻
分享
一粒白米飯
夠了　吃飽了

竹筍

殼

裡面　也是殼

殼裡面　還是殼

殼裡面的裡面　還是殼

由大而小

一層層地小上去

剝　剝　剝

剝出了小小金字塔

爺爺會不會寂寞

媽媽不在
爸爸不在
姊姊不在
房子靜得咬人
我一個人在家

我會想
爺爺會不會寂寞
「奶奶會從天國回來
陪他說話嗎？」

想到這裡
我會打電話
跟爺爺說說話
房子有了「我的說話聲」
就靜不下來了

露珠

早晨
站在樹葉上
做早操的
露珠
朝陽露出慈柔的光芒
跟他說話
馬上露出七彩的
笑容

窗

小時候
窗是大自然的好朋友
告訴我
季節的訊息
小鳥唱著甜美的歌聲

長大了
窗戶長高了
卻綁著粗鐵條
大自然沉默的像
電視的臉

門，偷偷在哭泣！

拉開竹門的聲音
親切
按電鈴開門的聲音
刺耳
跟對講機講話的聲音
冷淡
使用刷卡的聲音
孤寂

從鑰匙到刷卡
大家的心
變得更加驚慌
害怕被偷
害怕被搶
甚至綁架
門
偷偷在哭泣

豹

一波一波
男男女女
一波一波
老老少少
瞪著大眼睛看我
凝視著我的眼睛
害怕的往後逃
大吼一聲
撞到了「鐵欄杆」

非洲的大草原
我是王
聽到吼聲
動物們逃得無影無蹤
敢瞧我一眼
一口吞進去
摸一摸撞到　的　額頭

眼淚一顆顆掉下來
天天躺著　站著
等待　大家參觀
好像是路邊攤的
玩具豹

駱駝

駱駝的背
馱著兩桶水

走過長長乾乾的
沙漠

渴了，摸一摸水桶
主人的眼睛
睜得比水桶大

加法與減法

孩子　你的生命
是加法
每一分　每一秒
都在成長

孩子　你不要太貪玩
否則　減法
在旁邊等待機會
偷你的時間

怪眼鏡

眼睛
非常羨慕
手能用筆

一筆一劃地寫
內心好想寫寫看

眼睛
期盼一副會寫字的
怪眼鏡

床

躺在床上
就會想到樹

樹站了一天
腳會不會痠

樹會不會想
躺下來睡覺呢？

颱風來了
樹才肯躺下來睡覺

車過水里

道路的兩旁都是樹
不是趾高氣昂的高樓大廈
坐在小巴的座位上
感覺自己是一隻蝴蝶
每一次看的眼睛
都想寫一首詩

車過信義鄉

一整片
一整片
的葡萄架
葡萄架下
一串串的葡萄
農夫為一串串
葡萄　穿上
美麗的小裙子

眼睛
告訴
舌頭
不用吃
就甜滋滋的

車過東埔小鎮

車過東埔小鎮的
街道　打開了
小時候的記憶　浮現
故鄉北斗鎮的街道
聞到了純樸的味道

轉大人

爬山的
爬
嬰兒學走路的
爬
爬山的心情
嬰兒學爬的心情

嬰兒爬久了
站起來
就會走路了
爬山，一步一步的
爬
爬上山頂
就會爬山了

花開花謝

花開了
時間也開了
時間有了影像

花謝了
時間也凋謝了
時間有了回憶
花開花謝
時間有了存在的陰影

笛子

笛子
有許多個嘴巴
每一個嘴巴
都會唱歌

只有一個嘴巴的我
卻可以吹出
笛子每一個嘴巴
會唱歌的歌曲

西瓜

追求圓滿
像太陽
學習熱情

剝開來
洋溢著
紅紅的熱情

皺紋 I

湖一定很老
丟下一個小石子
比老太婆還老

漸漸的
皺紋變少了
又變年輕了

玉蘭花

一朵花開了
一朵花開了
許多花開了

玉蘭花
開了許多花
風邀我一起香舞

大樹

大樹的心窗
不做鐵門
不做鐵窗

任隨陽光撒野
任隨東風搶劫
任隨小鳥做窩

蘭花開

花苞
奮力睜開
眼睛
不知
想看清楚什麼

曇花驚醒了酣睡的朝陽

藏在黑夜下
追求美的彩虹

不服輸的心　燃燒著
花開了　香味一縷縷
噴出　不服輸的心也綻開
像月亮一樣的花瓣

謝了　驚醒了
酣睡的朝陽

白千層

樹幹的皮膚不漂亮
樹葉非常秀氣
白頭翁和綠繡眼
一大早
就會到樹葉裡
舉行歌唱比賽

大門口
負責盡職的守衛
一秒鐘
也不敢離開
目送學生上學
目送學生放學
目送老師退休
目送校長離職
不知不覺
它是一本照相簿

黑色的鋼琴

活動中心
一架黑色的鋼琴
嚴肅的沉默
沉默的黑色
逼著眼睛注視
甚至打開琴蓋彈湊

不會彈琴的我
走過去的腳步是雀躍的
心裡很想打開琴蓋
彈奏一番
不會彈琴的事實
黑色的鋼琴成為遺憾的疤

鞋子

他，歡樂
留下的汗珠
他，悲傷
留下的淚珠
他，緊張
留下的汗珠
他，運動
留下的汗珠

鞋子
一滴滴的收藏著
為了給她讀
讀出歲月的滋味

對話

蟬在樹梢唱歌
質問，冷氣機
你為什麼要發出怪聲

冷氣機
反問蟬
你為誰唱歌

蟬
反而唱得
更大聲

小陽傘

小山羊說
我好想撐陽傘

小草說
我不能當你的陽傘

姑婆芋說
我也不能當你的陽傘

小紅傘說
我也不想當你的陽傘

小雲朵說
我願意當你的小洋傘

坐在鞦韆上

坐在鞦韆上
就像擁有一對翅膀
向小鳥學習飛翔
享受飛翔的樂趣
小鳥用翅膀　飛翔
我用腳當翅膀　飛翔
雙腳用力一盪
飛在半空中　眼睛
不敢往下看
飛在空中的小鳥
不知會不會害怕

坐在鞦韆上
飛上飛下的感覺
就像一隻飛翔的小鳥
將快樂的心情交給風去傳播

籃筐與專櫃小姐

每次走入百貨公司
看見坐在椅子上的專櫃小姐
就想起　籃球架的籃框
也是這般地等待
像一隻懶貓
籃框也是一樣
有人來投籃
臉像一朵綻開的花瓣

籃球是我的好朋友

籃球是一粒大蘋果
張開雙手擁抱
手指頭大喊　痛

體育老師告訴我
跟籃球擁抱的方法
籃球漸漸成為我的好朋友

他每次看到我
露出紅紅的笑容
我也露出白白的笑容

操場

坐下來　伸出巨大的
手掌
等待大家來運動
大家流汗的汗珠
是我最珍愛的珍珠
大家的最愛
也是我的最愛

坐下來　一個比湖大的
水平面
小朋友
是一條條快活的魚

跑步 I

每次跑步的時候
就會思考一個問題
手會不會罵腳太慢
腳會不會罵手太慢

世界百米金牌選手
手腳一定相處得非常和睦
從來不爭吵的
從來不爭功的

每次跑步的時候
就會反省自己
如何讓自己跟妹妹
和睦相處

剪草機

牛馬羊
不吃汽油的剪草機
一口又一口的剪草
日出日落

天黑了
睡夢中
身體一點又一點的
膨脹
有時也會生下一個
小生命

天亮了
大草原綠出青又輕又青的
笑容
歡迎他們

書法家

風
拿出巨大的毛筆
沾著綠色的綠汁
在草原上
寫了一個巨大的漢字
無
讓太陽、白雲、老鷹閱讀

蒙古包

蒙古包
你會寂寞嗎

牛馬羊
陪伴在你身旁
日出　喜樂咀嚼草原
日落　舒適斜躺睡覺

皺紋 II

山
溫柔的胸懷
等待
遠方　歸來
的白雲

每一條曲線
都是
擔憂的
皺紋

門

早上全家出門
門緊閉著嘴巴
下午放學回家
門大喊一聲回家

晚上出門補習
門皺著眉頭

夜深補習回家
門正在做甜夢

線

天地之間不會相撞
一定有一條線撐著

太陽東升西落
一定有一條線撐著

生命不斷成長
一定有一條線撐著

父母愛子女的心
一定有一條線撐著

燭

夜　木炭的黑
守著黑黑的孤獨

燭光　　聆聽
夜黑黑的心聲

燭光　　打開
夜黑黑的心靈

燭光　　窺見
夜黑黑的眼睛

弦

有一條弦
扣緊心情

愉快的心情
弦　悠然自得

煩惱的心情
弦　緊鬆不定

沉思的心情
慵懶的小貓

好母親

阿嬤
每次拜拜
拿著香，喃喃自語
說個不停
仔細一聽
每次的內容都一樣
猜想
神明聽久了
也會變成一位好母親

為日本兒童祈禱

大海
請你不要再怒吼了
我的家屋　被捲走了
我的田園　被捲走了
我的書包　被捲走了

土地
請你不要再搖晃了
道路　搖塌了
牆壁　搖裂了
高樓搖倒了

太陽請你趕快把陽光灑落大地
安慰受傷的動植物
關懷震壞的家園
傾聽哭泣的兒童

星月
請你不要再躲起來
請你把亮光
點亮整個天空
照亮每一個悲傷的人

雪花
請你們不要再飄落了
請你們趕快融化
流入河川
流入田園
流入兒童哭泣的心

春風
請你坐著魔毯
把希望送給每位兒童

把勇氣放入兒童的心靈
喚醒兒童雀躍的心情

天空在遠方招手
耶穌在遠方招手
佛陀在遠方招手
阿拉在遠方招手
媽祖在遠方招手

我是一粒籃球

我是一粒籃球
只有一樣本領
彈彈跳跳
還有一顆馬上服務的心

籃球比賽的時候
我是最佳男主角
觀眾的眼睛緊盯著我
害羞的臉變紅

我是一粒籃球
看到小朋友
玩得開心
彈跳得　更開心

跑步 II

坐著不動的
操場
露出慈祥的
笑容
跟著他圓形的
肚子
跑完一圈後
呼吸不順暢
雙腳走不動

操場
坐著不動
肚子一圈圈的
皺紋
鼓勵大家
繼續跑就不累了

乒乓球

一張桌子
一張網子
一雙拍子
一粒白球
雙方殺得眼花撩亂
汗流浹背

不管誰贏

一張桌子仍然一張桌子
一張網子仍然一張網子
一隻拍子仍然一隻拍子
一粒白球仍然一粒白球

羽球

沒有自己的主張
隨著兩方的對手
打過來打過去
也不敢叫累

有一點　他不明白
觀眾看到他落地
響起如雷的掌聲
那一刻是他休息的時候

我會飛了

蟬蛹由地底下
鑽出來
爬上樹幹
從蛹的中央裂縫
張開潮濕的翅膀
飛的意志喊痛
風趕緊用愛吹乾

飛上樹梢
用力吶喊
我會飛了　樹聽到了嗎
我會飛了　樹聽到了嗎

Formosa

畫Formosa
要用許多顏色

用土地的顏色
用高山的顏色
用大海的顏色
用陽光的顏色
用黑夜的顏色
用月亮的顏色
用風雨的顏色
用四季的顏色
……
我要用管芒草的筆
我要用一輩子的時間
畫一幅Formosa

作者介紹

　　蔡榮勇，1955年出生於台灣彰化縣北斗鎮，台中師專畢業。現為笠詩社社務兼編輯委員、台灣現代詩人協會理事、世界詩人組織（PPDM）會員。曾出版詩集《生命的美學》、《洗衣婦》及合集多種。2009年曾赴蒙古參加台蒙詩歌交流，2014年分別參加在古巴及智利舉行的國際詩歌節。

英文譯者介紹

　　陳郁青，政大財務管理系學士。參加中國生產力中心培訓後進入了翻譯的世界，成為中英口、筆譯者。因為想旁聽法律英文課，意外成為法律研究生，在學中。通過理解不同的語言，豐富自己的生命與視野。

日文譯者介紹

　　保坂登志子，1937年出生於日本東京。國學院大學中國文學系碩士。譯著：《海流 I・II・III 日本・台灣兒童詩對譯選集》、《台灣平埔族傳說》、短篇小說集《獵女犯》、《台灣民間故事》。詩集五本、評論集一本。1992年創刊*Kodama*《回聲》（世界成人和兒童詩誌）。日本翻譯家協會理事、日本詩人Club會員。

【英語篇】
Thank you Diary

Acknowledgments

To bridge cultures between Taiwan and Japan, poetess Hosaka Tosiko (1937-) has translated Taiwanese poems for children and published in *ECHO* and *Blue Earth*.

From 1990 to 2019, she translated my poems , in a total number of 50, and I am not sure if I missed any.

Japanese is Greek to me and I feel so embarrassed that she always wrote me Chinese letters with her beautiful handwriting.

She visited Taiwan about four times, and in each of our meetings, we communicated in written Chinese.

Every time, I made up my mind learning Japanese but ended up quitting.

So I complied these poems for publication to express my gratitude in return for her appreciation.

日記，謝謝你

Thank you Diary・日記よ、ありがとう

CONTENTS

目次
CONTENTS

日記，謝謝你

Thank you Diary・日記よ、ありがとう

Thank you Diary

Thank you Diary

You put up with my selfishness

You ease my sorrow

You tolerate my anger

You compliment my cheerfulness

……

Thank you Diary

For collecting

My true colors

A Grain of Rice

A grain of rice

Takes several dozens of ants to lift up

For a meal, I have

Several thousand grains of rice

Several dozens of ants

Share

A grain of rice

Enough, I am full

Bamboo Shoots

The tough leaf

Inside is also the tough leaf

Inside the tough leaf are still tough leaves

Inside the inside of tough leaves is still the tough leaf

From big to small

It gets smaller and smaller layer after layer

Peel peel peel

Voila A small pyramid

Is Grandpa Going to be Lonely

Mom is not around

Dad is not around

Elder sister is not around

The house is dauntingly quiet

I am at home alone

I would wonder

Is Grandpa going to be alone

"Would Grandma come back from heaven

And talk with him?"

Thinking of this

I make a call

To talk with Grandpa

When the house is filled with "my sound of chatters"

It is no longer quiet

Dew

In the morning
The dew
Standing on the leaves
Does morning exercises
The morning sun shines tenderly
To talk to it
Which reveals a rainbow-like
Smile

The Window

When I was little

The window was the good friend of Mother Nature

Telling me

The messages of the seasons

The birds sang beautifully

I grew up

The window grew taller

But is tied with thick iron bars

The Mother Nature is as silent as

The face of the television

The Door, Weeping Surrentitiously!

The sound of opening the bamboo door
Is friendly
The sound of ringing the doorbell
Is cacophonous
The sound talking to the intercom
Is cold
The sound of swiping the card
Is lonely

From the key to the card
People
Get more scared of
Being stolen
Being mugged
Even being kidnapped
The Door
is weeping surreptitiously

Leopard

Wave after wave of

Men and women

Wave after wave of

Senior and junior people

Stare at me with their wide open eyes

And gaze at my eyes

I fearfully flee backwards

Howl loudly

And hit the "iron bars"

In the African savanna

I am the king

When hearing my roars

Animals flee without a trace

Those dare to look at me

I would swallow them in one gulp

I touch the forehead that was hit

One after one teardrop falls down

Lying or standing every day

I wait to be visited

Like the toy leopard

In the market stall

Camels

The hunch of camels
Carries two buckets of water

The camels walk through the long and dry
Desert

When thirsty, touching the buckets
The master has his eyes open
Bigger than the bucket

Addition and Subtraction

Child   Your life
Is addition

Each minute   Each second
You are growing up

Child   Don't be too playful
Otherwise subtraction
Is waiting by your side
To steal your time

A Pair of Weird Glasses

Eyes

Envy

Hands which can use the pen

To write each and every stroke

They want to try writing themselves

Eyes

Expect to depend on

A Pair of Weird Glasses that writes

The Bed

Lying on the bed
I always think of trees

Trees stand a long day
Do they have leg pain

Do trees want to
Lie down to sleep

Only when typhoon hits
Trees will lie down to sleep

The Car Passing by Shuili

Trees, not the haughty buildings and skyscrapers

Stand on both sides of the roads

Sitting in the small bus

I felt I were a butterfly

My eyes that watch every time

Would like to write a poem

The Car Passing by Xinyi Township

A stretch of

A stretch of

Canopy for grapes

Under the canopy are

Clusters of grapes

Farmers have clusters of

Grapes wear

Beautiful little skirts

The eyes

Tell

The tongue

You don't have to taste

to know its lovely sweetness

The Car Passing
by Dongpu Small Town

The Car Passing by Dongpu Small Town

The streets open up

My childhood memories   The emergence

of the streets in my hometown Beidou Township

I smell of the smell of simplicity

Growing up

Crawling

When I go mountain climbing

Crawling

When a toddler learns to walk

The mood when I go mountain climbing

The mood when a baby's learning to crawl

A baby crawls long enough

As soon as it stands up

It can walk

Mountain climbing, step by step

When going mountain climbing

At the mountain top

You know how to climb a mountain

Flowers Bloom and Wither

Flowers are blooming

So is time

And time has its image

Flowers are withering

So is time

And time has its memory

Flowers Bloom and Wither

And time has the shadow of existence

A Flute

A flute
has many mouths
Each mouth
Can sing

I have only one mouth
But I can play
The songs
Each mouth of the flute can sing

Watermelons

In pursuit of fulfillment
Like the sun
It learns to be passionate

Opened up
It brims with
The passion of red

Wrinkles I

The lake must be old

When a pebble is thrown in it

It gets older than an old woman

Gradually

The wrinkles are fewer

It is rejuvenated

Mangnolia

A flower is in full bloom
A flower is in full bloom
Many flowers are in full bloom

Mangnolia
is in full bloom with many flowers
The wind invites me to dance together in the fragrance

A Big Tree

The heart of a big tree is like a window

It doesn't require an iron door

It doesn't require the iron grating

Let the unbridled sunshine be

Let the east wind loot

Let the birds nest

The Blooming Orchid

Its buds

Strive to open up

The eyes

I wonder

What they want to see

Epiphyllum Wakes up the Early Sun that Sleeps Soundly in Shock

Hidden in the dark night
The rainbow pursues the delicacy

The heart that yields to none is blazing
The flower is in full bloom with wisps of scents
Giving out   The heart that yields to none also opens up
The petals are like the moon

Its withering away wakes up
The early sun that is in a sound sleep

Melaleuca

The skin of the trunk is not pretty
The foliage is very fine
Chinese bulbuls and Japanese White-eyes
Have their singing contest
In the tree
In the early morning

The gate
A responsible and dutiful security guard
Dares not to leave
A second
Seeing students go to school
Seeing students leave school
Seeing teachers get retired
Seeing the school principal leave her job
Unwittingly
It is a photo album

The Black Piano

In the activity center

Stands a black piano

Solemn silence

Silent black

Forces the eyes to watch it

Even opens the fall board to play

I don't know how to play the piano

Light-footed walking towards it

I wanted to open the fall board

And played the piano

The fact that I don't know how to play

The black piano becomes the scar of regret

Shoes

He, with delight

Left beads of sweat

He, in sorrow

Left beads of tears

He, highly strung

Left beads of sweat

He, working out

Left beads of sweat

Shoes

Collect each and every bead

In order to read her

the taste of time

Dialog

Cicadas on the twigs sing

Asking the air conditioner

Why do you make strange sounds

The air conditioner

Counter asked cicadas

Who do you sing for

And cicadas

Sing

Even much louder

The Little Parasol

The little goat said
I wanted badly to carry a parasol

The little grass said
I can't be your parasol

The giant taro said
I can't be your parasol, either

The little red brolly said
I don't want to be your parasol, either

The little cloud said
I am willing to be your little parasol

Sitting on the swing

Sitting on the swing
Is like having a pair of wings
Learning to fly like a bird
Enjoying the fun of flying
The bird uses its wings to fly
I use my legs as wings to fly
Pumping my legs on a swing
in the mid air I dare not
Look down
Birds flying in the sky
I wonder if they are afraid

Sitting on the Swing
Flying up and down
Is like a flying bird
Let the wind spread its joy

Basketball Hoop and the Sales Lady

Every time I walk into a department store

Seeing the sales lady sitting on the chair

I would think of the basketball hoop attached to the stand

Waiting as such

Like a lazy cat

The hoop is the same

Someone comes to shoot

And its face is like a blooming petal

Basketball is My Best Friend

Basketball is a big apple

Opening my arms to hug it

My fingers cried   Ouch

My PE teacher told me

How to hug a basketball

Basketball gradually becomes my good friend

Whenever it sees me

It has a red smile

And I also wear a white smile

Sports Field

Sitting down Reaching out my giant

Palm

Waiting all to come exercise

All's beads of sweat

are my favorite pearls

All's favorite

Is also mine

Sitting down The water level

Bigger than a lake

Children

Are a school of cheerful fish

Jogging I

Whenever I jog
I think of a question
Whether my hands would blame my feet for being too slow
Whether my feet would blame my hands for being too slow

The gold medalist of the world 100 meter dash
Must have his hands and feet get along very well
They never quarrel
They never fight for credits

Whenever I jog
I reflect on myself
How to get along with my sister
Well

Lawnmowers

Cows, horses and goats are

Lawnmowers that don't need gasoline

Bite after bite to mow the lawn

Sun rises and sun sets

It is dark

In my dream

My body expanded

Bit by bit

Sometimes it is

Another new life

It is dawn

The grassland welcomes them

With a smile that is

Green and bright and green

A Calligrapher

Wind
Takes out a gigantic brush pen
Dipped with green ink
On the grassland and
Write a huge Chinese character
NIL
For Sun, clouds, and eagles to read

Yurt

Yurt

Are you lonely

Cows, horses and goats

Accompany you

At sunrise They graze happily on pastures

At sunset They snugly recline and sleep

Wrinkles II

Mountains
whose gentle bosoms
Wait for
The white clouds
Coming back from afar

Each curve
Is
A fretting
Wrinkle

The Door

After the whole family go out in the morning
The door firmly shuts its mouth
When I come home after school in the afternoon
The door makes a loud shout HOME

I go to cram school in the evening
And the door frowns

As I come home from cram school in the dark night
The door is having a sweet dream

Strings

Heaven and earth don't collide with each other
There must be a string pulling

The sun rises in the east and sets in the west
There must be a string pulling

We continue to grow
There must be a string pulling

Parents love their children
There must be a string pulling

Candles

The charcol dark night
Stands by the dark loneliness

The candle light listens to
The voice of the the dark night

The candle light inspires
The mind of the dark night

The candle light gets a glimpse of
The eyes of the dark night

A String

There is a string
Fastening the emotions

The happy mood
The string is laid back

The worried mood
The string swings between tightness and looseness

The contemplative mood
A lazy kittie

A Good Mother

Nana

Whenever praying

She holds the incense and murmurs

Nonstop

Listen closely

The content is the same every time

I guess

When the deity listens long enough

SHE will also be a good mother

Pray for kids in Japan

Ocean

Please stop roaring angrily

My house   Washed away

My farmland   Washed away

My schoolbag   Washed away

Land

Please do not tremble anymore

The roads   Ruined

The walls   Broken

The buildings   Felt Apart

Sun please quickly shine on the earth

To comfort the injured fauna and flora

To care for the damaged homeland

To listen to the crying children

Stars and the moon

Please don't hide away any longer

Please let your light

Light up the whole sky

Light up every sorrowful being

Snow

Please stop falling down

Please quickly melt away

Flow into the rivers

Flow into the farmlands

Flow into children's weeping hearts

Spring breeze

Please be the blankets shielding against demons

And send hopes to every child

Put courage into the children's minds and
Wake up the children's frolic mood

The sky is waving its hand in distance
Jesus is waving his hand in distance
Buddha is waving his hand in distance
Allah is waving his hand in distance
Mazu is waving her hand in distance

I am a Basketball

I am a basketball

I have only one skill

Bouncing and jumping

And a heart readily to serve

During basketball games

I am the best leading actor

The audiences' eyes fixate on me

My shyness brings a blush to my cheeks

I am a basketball

When seeing children

Having fun

I jump and bounce even much happily

Jogging II

The sedentary
Sports field
Beams with a kind
Smile
Following his round
belly
I finished jogging a lap
I couldn't catch my breath
My legs couldn't move

Sports field
Sits still
Its belly has circles of
Wrinkles
Encouraging all
To keep running so the tiredness is away

Pingpong

A table

A net

A pair of bats

A white ball

The players hit the ball and make its flight hard to track

Both players sweat heavily

Whoever wins

A table is still a table

A net is still a net

A bat is still a bat

A white ball is still a white ball

Badminton

Without its own proposition
Following the players on both ends
Flighting here flighting there
It dares not to utter its tiredness

One thing it doesn't understand
When audiences see it fall down
The thunder like applause activates
The moment it rests

I Can Fly

The nymph in the soil

Climbs out

Climbs up to the tree trunk

From the cleavage of the nymph center

Unfurls the wet wings

Its will of flying cries hurt

The wind quickly uses love to dry them up

Flying up to the treetop

Roaring with force

I can fly　Does the tree hear me

I can fly　Does the tree hear me

Formosa

Painting Formosa
Needs many colors

The colors of the soil
The colors of the mountains
The colors of the ocean
The colors of the sunshine
The colors of the dark night
The colors of the moon
The colors of wind and rain
The colors of four seasons
......
I am going to use the miscanthus pen
I am going to use a lifetime
To paint a Formosa

About the Author

Tsai Jung-Yung was born in Beidou, Changhua County, Taiwan in 1955. After graduating from Taichung Teachers' College, He went to Mongolia on the poetry exchange between Taiwan and Mongolia in 2009. He attended International Poetry Festivals respectively in Cuba and Chile in 2014.He is currently an editing member of Li Poetry Group, a director in Taiwan Modern Poets' Association, and a member of PPDM.

About the English Translator

Jean Chen, graduated from College of Commerce, National Chengchi University, starts her translation journey upon finishing the translation and interpretation training in China Productivity Center in Taipei. Now she is serendipitously a full-time law school student; at first she was thinking to audit legal English only. Her life is enriched and horizon broadened through the learning of different languages.

About the Japanese Translator

Hosaka Tosiko was born in Tokyo in 1937 and graduated with a Master's degree from the Department ok Chinese Literature of the Kokugakuin University. Her translation work includes *The Ocean Current I, II, and III trilogy* (Anthologies of Taiwan and Japanese Children's Poems Translated to Chinese or Japanese), *The Legend of Taiwan's Pingpu Tribe,* and the anthologies of short stories *Hunting Captive Women* and *Taiwanese Folklores.* She has published five poem collections and one book on literary criticism. In 1992, she published the first issue of the global adults and children poetry magazine *Kodama.* She is on the board of the Japan Society of Translators and a member of the Japanese Poets Club.

【日語篇】
日記よ、ありがとう

ありがとう

　日台交流。女性詩人保坂登志子氏（1937-）は台湾の子どもの詩を翻訳し、『こだま詩選集』や『青い地球』で発表していらっしゃいます。大人と子どもに向けて創作していらっしゃいます。

　1990年から2019年にかけて、拙詩を少しずつ翻訳してくださり、把握しているのは50編あり、あるいは見落とされたものもあるかもしれませんが。

　私は日本語がわからないので、実に恥ずかしい話ですが、保坂氏からはいつも達筆な中国語で書かれた手紙をいただいております。台湾にいらっしゃったのは四回ほどですが、お会いした時には、いつも筆談でコミュニケーションをとっていました。日本語を勉強しようと幾度も決意したものの、いつも途中で諦めてしまいました。

　保坂氏のご厚意にお応えすべく、この度出版することに致しました。ささやかながら、この詩集を以って感謝の意を表したいと存じます。

日記，謝謝你
Thank you Diary・日記よ、ありがとう

目次

日記，謝謝你

Thank you Diary・日記よ、ありがとう

日記よ、ありがとう

日記よ、ありがとう！
あなたは　私のわがままを許してくれる
あなたは　私の悲しみを晴らしてくれる
あなたは　私の腹立ちを受け入れてくれ
あなたは　楽しい私を喜んでくれる
……
日記よ
ありがとう！
あなたは
うそや飾りのない私をしまっておいてくれる

一粒の白米飯

一粒のご飯を
何十匹ものアリが引っぱって動かしている
僕は一晩に
何千粒もの
白米ご飯を食べる
何十匹ものありは　分かち合って
一粒の白米飯で
満腹した　おいしかったと

たけのこ

硬い皮
内側も硬い
硬い内側はまだ硬い
大きい皮からだんだん小さく
ますます小さく上がっていく
はぐ　はぐ　はぐ
はいで　現れたのは小さな金字塔（ピラミット）

金字塔：ピラミットのこと。形が金の字に似ていること
からいう。

おじいちゃんはさびしくないのかな

お母さんはるす
お父さんはるす
お兄さんもお姉さんもいない
私は一人で家にいる
家は静まりかえって何だかぞーっとする

私はふっと思う
おじいちゃんはさびしくないのかな
「おばあちゃんが天国から帰って來て
おじいちゃんの話しあいてをするのかな」

それで私は
おじいちゃんに電話して
話をすることを思いついた
そうすれば部屋は「私の話し声」がして
静まりかえってしまうことはないもの

つゆの珠（たま）

朝
木の葉の上で
早朝体操をしている
つゆ
やさしい朝の光と
話をしている
あっ
七色の笑顔を見せた

窓

幼い頃
窓は大自然のよい友だちだった
私に
季節の息づかいを教え
小鳥は心地よいうたを歌っていた

大人になったら
窓は高くなって
太い鉄線でしばられ
大自然は
黙り込んでいるテレビの顔みたいになった

ドアは隱（かく）れて泣いている

竹のドアを開ける時の音は
親しみがもてます
ベルを押してドアを開ける時の音は
耳ざわりです
対話器に向かって話す時の声は
冷たいです
カードを通す時の音は
さびしいです

カギからカードまで
みんなの心は
驚きあわてるようになって
盗まれるのをこわがり
奪（うば）われるのをこわがり
はなはだしい時は拉致（らち）されることさえあります
ドアは
隠れて泣いています

豹

波のようにおしよせる
男たち女たち
波のようにおしよせる
老人たち子どもたち
大きな目でおれを見ている
おれの目をじっと見つめている
おれはこわくなって後ずさり
大きく一ほえしたら
ドスン！鉄さくにぶつかった

アフリカの大草原では
おれは王様だ
おれのほえ声を聞けば
動物たちはにげ　かげをひそめ
おれをひと目見返そうものなら
ひと飲みにしてしまう

ぶつけたあたまをさすると
目からなみだがぼろばろ落ちる
毎日ねそべったり　立ち上がったり
みんなが見に來るのを　待っている
まるで道ばたにならべて売っている
おもちゃの豹さ

らくだ

らくだの背には
二つの水桶を乗せている

長いこと
乾いた砂漠を歩いた

のどが渇いて　水桶をさわったら
主人は目を
水桶よりも大きく見張っている

たし算とひき算

子どもよ　君のいのちは
たし算です
一分　一秒ごとに
成長していく

子どもよ　あまり遊びすぎてはいけないよ
ひき算は
君のそばにいて
君の時間を盗むチャンスをねらっているよ

魔法めがね

目は
手が筆を上手に使えるのが
とてもうらやましい

一筆一画　書ける手
目は自分も書いてみたいなあと思っている

目は
字が書ける
魔法のめがねがとっても欲しい

ベッド

ベッドに横たわると
すぐ木のことを思う

木は一日中つっ立っていて
足がつかれないのかな？

木は横になって寝たいと
思わないのかな？

台風が來たら　木はようやく
地面に横になって寝ることにした

車は水の里を通る

道の両側は樹だ
それは得意満面な高層ビルではない
小型バスの座席に座っている自分は
一匹の蝶だ
初めて目に映るもの
すべてが詩だ

車は義郷を通る

過不足なく
過不足なく
葡萄棚の
棚の下に
一房　一房　葡萄が連なっている
農夫が一房ずつ
葡萄に
きれいなスカートを穿（は）かせている

目が
語っている
舌を使わなくても
それがとても甘いことを

車は東埔の街を通る

車が東埔の小村を通ると
街道が　思い出させる
幼い頃の記憶が　浮かび上がった
故郷北斗村の街道
純朴な匂いがしてきた

大人になる

山にのぼる　の
のぼる という字は
赤ちゃんがハイハイするの
はう（爬）という字だ

山にのほる気持は
赤ちゃんがハイハイする気持ちだ

赤ちゃんはしばらくハイハイしてから
立ち上がり
歩くことができる

山のほりは　一歩一歩
爬って歩き
山頂に爬い上がる

山頂に爬い上がることが
つまり山に登ることができたことなんだ

註:山に登る、の華語は「爬山」と書く。「爬」は爪をかけては
　　って歩く意。

花咲き花散る

花が咲いた
時間も咲いた
時間には映像があった

花が萎（しお）れ
時間も萎れた
時間には想い出があった

花は咲き花は散り
時間には存在した映像があった

笛

笛には
たくさんの口があり
その一つ一つが
歌えます

たった一つの口しかない私でも
たくさんの口が歌う
それぞれの笛の歌を
歌えるんですよ

スイカ

スイカは円を追求し
太陽に向かって
熱心に学習している

切り開いてみれば
赤い情熱が
あふれている

皺（しわ）Ⅰ

湖はきっと年をとっているのだ
小石を投げたら.
どんどん老いてお婆さんになった

やがてだんだんに
皺が少なくなって
又若返った

玉蘭ぎよくらん

一輪咲き
一輪咲き
たくさん咲いた

玉蘭の樹は
満開になった
風が私を誘い一緒に仲良く踊った

大樹

大樹の心の窓は
鉄の戸は作らず
鉄の窓は作らない

太陽の思いのままに開放し
春風の襲いかかるまま
小鳥が巣を作るに任せている

蘭

つぼみは
いっしょうけんめい目を開けようとしている
あけた目で
いったい
何をみきわめたいんだろう

月下美人草はお陽様（ひさま）を起こした

夜のやみにかくれて
美しい虹を追い求めている

ひけをとるまいと　情熱をもやし
開いた花の　香りがただよう
ひめていた　負けまいとする思いはほころび
月のような花びらが開いた

ぐっすりねむっていたお陽様は
びっくりして　目をさました

苦労重ね

幹の肌（はだ）はきれいじゃないが
木の葉はとても美しい
ムクドリとメジロが
朝早くから
葉のしげみの中で
歌大会をやっている

彼は校門に立っている
守衛さん
一秒も
門から離れず
学生の登校を見守り
下校を見送り
先生の定年退職（ていねんたいしょく）を
また校長の退職を見とどけ
いつの間にか
一冊（いっさつ）のアルバムになっている

黒いピアノ

スポーツセンターには
黒いピアノが一台
おごそかに沈黙している
黙り込んでいる黒に
目を奪われ
ピアノのふたを開け弾いてみたくなった

ピアノを弾けない私は
そばに行き

どきどきしながらふたを開け
鍵盤をたたいてみたいのだが
ピアノを弾けない事実で
黒いピアノは悔しい傷跡になってしまった

くつ

彼（かれ）が　楽しんで流した
汗（あせ）
彼が　悲（かな）しんで流した
涙（なみだ）
彼が緊張（きんちょう）して流した
汗
彼が運動で流した
汗

くつが
その一滴一滴（いってきいってき）をしまっているのは
彼にそれを読ませて
歳月（さいげつ）のいとおしさをわからせたいからだ

対話

木の梢で歌っている蝉が
質問しました　冷房機に
あなたはどうして奇妙な音を出すのですか

冷房機は
問い返しました
あなたは誰のために歌っているのですか

蝉は
歌を
更に大声で歌いました

小さな日傘

小ヤギは対いました
わたしは日傘を張っているみたいだ

小さな草か言いました
わたしはあなたの日傘になれません

サトイモが言いました
わたしもあなたの日傘になれません

小さな紅い傘も言いました
わたしもあなたの日傘になれません

小さな雲が言いました
わたしはあなたの小さな日傘になりたいです

ブランコにのる

ブランコに乗ると
まるで一対の羽があるみたい
小鳥が飛ぶ練習をしているように
飛ぶ楽しさがわかる

小鳥は羽を使って　飛び
ぼくは脚（あし）を羽にして　飛ぶ
両脚に力をいれてこぎ
空中に飛ぶと　目は
下を見るのがこわい
空を飛ぶ小鳥は
怖（こわ）いことがあるのかしら

ブランコに乗って
上に下に飛ぶ気持は
一羽の飛ぶ鳥のようだと
楽しい気持を風に伝えさせよう

バスケットと案内専門の女性

いつもデパートに入ると
椅子に座っている案内専門（せんもん）の女性を見て
すぐにバスケットボールのバスケットのことを思い出す
バスケットもこんな風に待っているんだ
まるでなまけ猫みたいに
バスケットだって
人がボールをシュートすれば
顔が花びらのようにほころびるもの

バスケットボールはぼくの好い友だち

バスケットボールは大きいりんごだ
両手でかかえようとすると
指が大声で叫ぶ　痛い

体育の先生に
バスケットボールのかかえ方を教わったので
バスケットボールはだんだん
ぼくの好い友だちになった

かれはいつもぼくに会うと
赤い笑顔をし
ぼくも白い笑顔をする

運動場

座ったまま　差し出している大きな
手のひらで
みんなを待っている運動場です
みんなが流す汗は
わたしの一番大切な真珠です
みんなが一番好きなことは
わたしも一番好きなことです

座ったまま　湖みたいに大きな
水面にいる
小さいお友だちは
一匹一匹が活発な魚です

ランニング

いつも走っている時
こんなことを考える
手は脚（あし）が遅いと悪口を言えるか
脚は手が遅いと悪口を言えるか

世界の百メートル金メダル選手は
手脚がきっととても仲良しで
口争いもせず
手柄（てがら）を争うこともないのでしょう

いつも走っている時
自己反省する
どうしたら自分は妹と
仲良くできるんだろうと

草刈機

牛馬羊は
機械で刈った草を食べません
ひとくち　ひとくち草をかみ切り
日の出から日暮れまで

日が暮れれば
ぐっすり眠り
体はちょっとずつ
ふくらんで
時に小さないのちを
生みます

夜が明けると
大草原は青々として、
ニコニコ顔で
彼らを迎えます

書家

風は
巨大な毛筆で
緑の緑汁をうるおし
草原に
一字　巨大な字を書きました
無
太陽、雲、タカに読ませるために

モンゴルのパオ

モンゴルのパオは
寂しいことがありましょうか

牛馬羊が
あなたのそばにつきそい
日が昇れば　楽しく草をはみ
日が沈めば　気持ちよく眠ります

皺（しわ）II

山は
ふところ
おだやかな懐（ふところ）で
遠くから帰ってくる
白雲を
待っています

山の曲線は
みな
心配してできた
しわです

門

朝家族は門を出る
門はしっかり口を閉ざしている

午後学校が終わって帰ってくると
門は大声でお帰りと叫ぶ

夕方補習に出かけると
門は眉間（みけん）にしわを寄せている

夜遅く補習から帰ってくると
門は甘い夢を見ている

線

天と地はぶつかるはずがない
そこには必ず一本の線が支えているから

太陽は東に昇り西に沈む
そこには必ず一本の線が引きあっている

命はたえず成長する
そこには必ず一本の線が伸びている

父母の子を愛する心
そこには必ず一本の線で繋（つな）がれている

蠟燭（ろうそく）

夜は　炭の黒
黒々と孤独を守っている

蠟燭（ろうそく）の光は
夜の真っ暗な心に耳傾けている

蠟燭の光は　開（あ）けた
夜の暗い心を

蠟燭の光は　ひそかに見ている
夜の黒い眼を

弦（げん）

一張りの弦は
心とぴったり合わせて奏（かな）でる

愉快な気持ちの時
弦は　ゆったり満足げに

悩みのある時
弦は　ゆるんで定まらない

物思いに沈んでいる時
弦は物ぐさな猫だ

良いお母さん

お母さんは
毎日拝んでいる
線香を手に　ナムナムと言いながら
となえ続けている
よく聞くと
いつも同じことを言っている
もしかしたら
神様がそれを聞き続けて
良いお母さんになったのかも知れない

日本のこどもたちに捧ぐ

海よ
どうかもう吼（ほ）えないで
私の家は　巻き上げられ
私の田畑は　巻きとられ
私のカバンも　巻き上げられた

地よ
どうかもう揺らさないで
道路は揺すり上げられ
壁は揺すり裂かれ
ビルは揺り倒された

太陽よ
早く陽光で大地を晒（さら）し
動植物が受けた傷を癒やして
壊れた家
泣いている子どもをなぐさめて

星と月よ
どうか寝ていないで起きて
明るい光を
空にともして
傷ついた人を照らして

雪よ
もう舞い落ちないでいい
早くとけて
河川を流れ
田畑を流れ
子どもの泣きたい心に流れて

春風よ
魔法のじゅうたんにのって
かわいいお友だちに送り届けてあげて

子どもの心に勇気を
子どもがわくわくするような春を

天の神さまは遠くから手を振り
イエスさまは遠くから手を振り
おしゃかさまは遠くから手を振り
アラーの神は遠くから手を振り
台湾のマソ神ははるかから
手を振っています

3・11東日本大震災お見舞い
台湾児童文学「満天星」編集者・詩友
蔡榮勇詩人より一国語日報児童文芸

ぼくはバスケットボール

ぼくはバスケットボール
得意ほただ一っ
跳ねること
ほかにサービス精神もある
バスケットの試合の時
ぼくはヒーロー
観客の目はじっとぼくを見つめるので
はずかしくて顔が赤くなる

ぼくはバスケットボール
小さい子が
楽しそうに遊んでいるのを見ると
ぼくはいよいよ楽しくなって跳ねる

走る

座ったまま動かない
グラウンドは
やさしい表情で
笑っこいる
くっついているのは
彼のまるいお腹
一回り走り終わって
呼吸はあらく
両足も動かない

グラウンドは
座ったまま動かない
お腹を取り巻く
皺もようが
走るのを続ければ梯れなくなるよと
みんなを励ましている

卓球

一面の台
一張りのネット
一組のラケット
一個の白ボ|ル
双方いそがしく目がかすみちらちらして
よく見えず　背中が汗でびっしよりだ

誰が勝つかに關わらず

台は依然として台
ネットは依然としてネット
ラケットは依然としてラケット
ポールはもとのままボールだ

バドミントン

自分の主張はない
両方の打ち手に従って
打たれて來て打たれて行き
疲れたと叫ぶ勇気もない

ちっとも 彼には解らなかった
観眾は彼が地に落ちるのを見て
雷のような拍手の音を響かせる
そのひと時が彼の休息の時間なのだとは

ぼくは飛べた

蝉の蛹は地下から
穴を開けて出てきて
樹の幹によじ登った
蛹の中央から裂いて
湿った羽を開いて
飛びたい気持で大声をあげると
風が急いで羽を優しく吹き乾かした

木の枝に跳び上がり
思い切り叫んだ
ぼく飛べたよ　樹たち聞こえた？
ぼく飛べたよ　樹たち聞こえた？

フォルモサ（麗しの島）

フォルモサを描くのは
沢山の色が必要だ

大地の色
高山の色
大海原の色
陽の光の色
夜
月明かりの色
雨風の色
四季の色
……

私わ芒の筆で
一生涯の時間をかけ
一幅のフォルモサの絵を描

著者について

　　蔡栄勇、1955年台湾彰化県北斗鎮生。台中師範専科学校卒
業。笠詩社の社務兼編集委員、台湾現代詩人協会理事、世界詩
人組織（PPDM）会員。詩集『命の美学（仮訳）』、『洗濯婦
（仮訳）』を出版、合著詩集も多数。2009年にはモンゴルへ台蒙
詩歌交流活動に、2014年にはキューバ、チリで開催されたポエト
リー・フェスティバルに参加。

英語訳者

　陳郁青、政治大学財務管理学科学士。中華民国（台湾）の
關連省庁が指導する「財団法人中国生產力センター」（CPC）で
訓練を経て、翻訳の世界に入り、英語・中国語の翻訳・通訳者
になった。法律關係の英文講義を傍聴したのをきっかけに、現
在法科大学院在学中。異なる言語を理解することで、人生と視
野を豊かにしたい。

日本語訳者

　保坂登志子、1937年東京生。1965年国学院大学大学院修士課程(中国文学専攻)修了。翻訳書『海流Ⅰ・Ⅰ・Ⅲ』日本・台湾成人と児童対訳詩集、『台灣平埔族的伝說』、短編小説集『猟女犯』、『台灣民間故事』。詩集五冊、評論一冊。1992年創刊『こだま』世界の成人と児童詩誌編集発行。日本翻訳家協会理事・日本詩人クラブ会員。

語言文學類　PG2754　台灣詩叢17

日記，謝謝你
Thank you Diary・日記よ、ありがとう
——蔡榮勇漢英日三語詩集

作　　　者／蔡榮勇（Tsai Jung-yung）
英語譯者／陳郁青（Jean Chen）
日語譯者／保坂登志子（Hosaka Tosiko）
叢書策劃／李魁賢（Lee Kuei-shien）
責任編輯／陳彥儒
圖文排版／陳彥妏
封面設計／王嵩賀

發 行 人／宋政坤
法律顧問／毛國樑　律師
出版發行／秀威資訊科技股份有限公司
　　　　　114台北市內湖區瑞光路76巷65號1樓
　　　　　電話：+886-2-2796-3638　傳真：+886-2-2796-1377
　　　　　http://www.showwe.com.tw
劃撥帳號／19563868　戶名：秀威資訊科技股份有限公司
　　　　　讀者服務信箱：service@showwe.com.tw
展售門市／國家書店（松江門市）
　　　　　104台北市中山區松江路209號1樓
　　　　　電話：+886-2-2518-0207　傳真：+886-2-2518-0778
網路訂購／秀威網路書店：https://store.showwe.tw
　　　　　國家網路書店：https://www.govbooks.com.tw

2022年6月　BOD一版
定價：260元
版權所有　翻印必究
本書如有缺頁、破損或裝訂錯誤，請寄回更換

讀者回函卡

國家圖書館出版品預行編目

日記,謝謝你:蔡榮勇漢英日三語詩集 = Thank
you diary = 日記よ、ありがとう/蔡榮勇著;
陳郁青英譯;保坂登志子日譯. -- 一版. -- 臺
北市:秀威資訊科技股份有限公司], 2022.06
　　面;　　公分. -- (語言文學類;PG2754)(台
灣詩叢;17)
　中英日對照
　BOD版
　ISBN 978-626-7088-61-6(平裝)

863.598　　　　　　　　　　　111005374